For the littlest loves of my life: Ben, Norah, & Henry

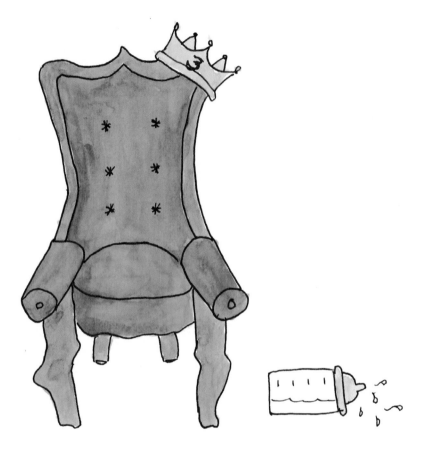

© 2022 Liz Doughty

ISBN: 978-1-66787-927-7

Edited by: Hilary Van Kuiken

Henry The Third

as told by Norah the Second

By: Liz Doughty

Illustrated by: Mary Ciaccio

My older brother, Ben, and I tried not to hover.

Mom and Dad brought him home wrapped in a blanket.

He smelled like soap and made lots of racket!

I asked Dad if we could play with him yet.

He said, "Not quite, but you can hold him if you sit!"

"Me first!" Ben said, always knowing what to do.

I've been the baby, though, and this is all pretty new.

I felt nervous to hold him. He's so tiny and loud!

But with Mom and Dad's help, now I know how.

Hold his head with my elbow; it's kind of heavy!

Keep gentle hands, but hug tighter if he's wiggly!

6

He peeked out of his blanket and to my surprise,
A head of brown hair and my blue eyes.

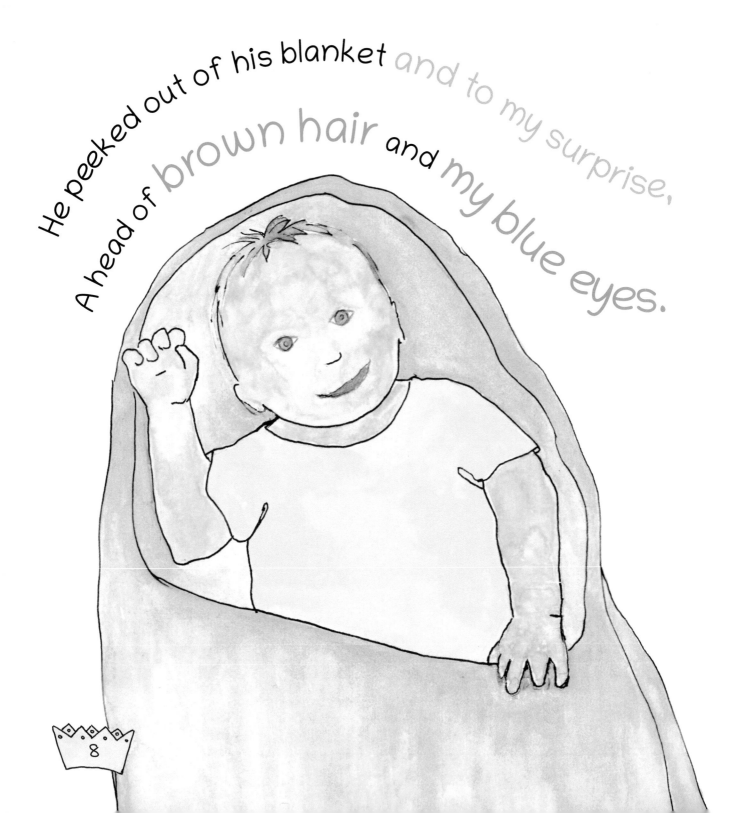

Dad thinks Henry has Ben's
button nose,

But Mom and I know he'll
look like me as he grows.

I'd been waiting for Henry to come for so long.

I'd have two brothers to play with rather than one!

But some of the changes don't feel all that good.

I'm not having the fun I thought I would.

10

Mom fed Henry instead of
putting me to bed,

And Dad had to bathe him
while we should've read.

11

Ben sang him songs when we usually play.

It feels like our family time is drifting away.

Dad must have noticed I felt a bit sad.

He asked,
"Norah, what's got you feeling so bad?"

I said I miss Mommy and playtime with Ben.

I wanted things just as they had always been.

He said, "You've been Mom's baby, right by her side.

Ben's been the biggest, leading as your guide.

But even with Henry here, Mom's hand is there to hold.

And like Ben has shown you, it's your turn to be bold."

"Me, the leader?" I wondered to myself,

Imagining reading Henry the books from my shelf.

And teaching him how to build a track for our trains,

Or sharing my puzzles, my dolls, and my games!

I'm a big sister now,
important, I know.

Now it's *my turn* to
help out with
my little bro.

Ben may be the oldest kid in our home,
But I'll be the best big sis the world's
ever known!

16

I have **lots** of big-sister jobs to do like

Handing Mom diapers and pacis, too.

I even help Henry get out his burps.

Rubbing his back or tummy
usually works!

Henry keeps growing a little every day.

I'm patiently waiting to teach him to play.

I don't have to worry I'll miss time with Mommy,

We will still spend time together as family.

Welcome to our family, Henry, welcome to our herd!

Mom, Dad, Ben the first, Me the second,

and Henry the third.